The
Weeks Hall
Tapes

compiled and annotated by
Morris Raphael

Morris Raphael 8-23-89
Best Wishes to Sara Richardson.
Hope you enjoy the book.
Morris

MORRIS RAPHAEL BOOKS
1404 Bayou Side Drive
New Iberia, Louisiana 70560

First Edition

Library of Congress Catalog Card No. 83-091286

ISBN 0-9608866-2-1

Portrait of Weeks Hall on front cover by Paul Gittings, Jr. Photo on back cover by Rose Anne Raphael.

Manufactured by Apollo Books Inc., 263 W. 5th St., Winona, MN 55987

PRINTED IN THE UNITED STATES OF AMERICA

Copies may be ordered from
MORRIS RAPHAEL BOOKS
1404 Bayou Side Drive
New Iberia, Louisiana 70560

In memory
of
my dear mother and father

PREFACE

This book represents a compilation of valuable observations by William Weeks Hall who is regarded as one of the South's most colorful aristocrats. He expired in 1958 and was the last private owner of that historic mansion, the Shadows-on-the-Teche, located in New Iberia, Louisiana.

Hall was a prominent New Iberia artist, art critic, photographer, gardener and lecturer. Somewhat of an eccentric, he became the sole owner of the famous antebellum home, the Shadows, in the early 1900's and spent a lifetime restoring it. The "Master of the Shadows" was the son of Gilbert Hall and Lily Weeks and the great-grandson of early pioneer David Weeks who built the Shadows.

Born Oct. 31, 1894 in New Orleans, Louisiana to elderly parents, Hall led a sheltered life as a young boy. He became a high school drop-out from the Old Boys' High School in New Orleans in the 10th grade. Although he had no extended formal education, he was considered a self-educated intellectual.

Hall won a scholarship in 1913 to attend the Pennsylvania Academy of Arts in Philadelphia, Pennsylvania. While at the Academy (1913-1915), he was awarded scholarships to study abroad in France and England. He deferred this activity until after World War I (Dec., 1920-May, 1922). During World War I he joined the U.S. Intelligence Service and served in a camouflage unit on the Gulf Coast. He was enrolled as Chief Petty Officer in the Navy in July, 1918 and received an honorable discharge December 20, 1918.

Hall's father died in 1909 and his mother died in 1918. As a result of their deaths, Hall developed a close relationship with his widowed aunt, Mrs. Walter Torian (nee Harriet

Weeks), who lived in New Orleans. When the salt mine structures at Weeks Island, Louisiana were destroyed by fire, Hall and his aunt sold their interest in the mine and paid off a mortgage which hung over the Shadows. Hall then bought out his aunt's half interest in the Shadows for $7,500 and became sole owner of the property.

In 1922, he secured the services of prominent New Orleans architect Richard Koch to restore the Shadows. Hall supervised the restoration of the gardens, and when the improvements were completed, the master of the Shadows invited famous artists, writers, and other professionals to visit his home and grounds.

In 1923, D. W. Griffith, famous movie director, was so impressed with the Shadows that he filmed "The White Rose" at the old home. The film featured Neil Hamilton and Mae Marsh. This led to the filming of portions of other movies at the Shadows.

Hall apparently fell in love with New Orleanian Fanny Craig who later married a Frenchman, Jacques Ventadour. He became despondent and began to drink heavily. He blamed himself for losing Miss Craig. A good friendship remained between the two, however. Hall reached his zenith as an artist in 1928 and his New Orleans exhibit of canvases received favorable response from art critics. His home and grounds and his reputation as a colorful entertainer attracted celebrities from all over the world. Famous visitors included Henry Miller, Lyle Saxon, Stark Young, Sherwood Anderson, Hodding Carter, Mae West, Joseph Cotten, Dick Powell, Cecil B. DeMille, Elia Kazan, Emily Post, Francis Biddle, the Lunts, Tex Ritter, and Kay Francis.

Weeks Hall heckled friends with late night telephone calls. He even tried calling the Pope and Adolph Hitler. He was a practical joker and played pranks on friends as well as on strangers.

Hall's right hand wrist was crushed in an automobile accident in 1935. He became handicapped as an artist and took up photography, pioneering in color transparencies. In later years he became more and more concerned about the welfare of the Shadows. In 1957, he appeared on Dave Garroway's nationally-televised show, "Wide, Wide World", where he made an appeal for some governmental agency to take over the Shadows. Hall received notification on his deathbed that the National Trust for Historic Preservation agreed to assume this responsibility. He died June 27, 1958.

Back in 1977, when I began research for writing a biography of Hall, The National Trust for Historic Preservation, which had accepted ownership of the Shadows, kindly allowed me the use of 39 tapes which Hall made in 1953. From all indications he had intended to write a cookbook, but I have no record that such a project was ever completed.

Although there were originally 44 tapes in the series, some evidently were lost, a few were erased, and several parts of the tapes were distorted. There was also some evidence of deterioration.

I took great pains to accurately transcribe these tapes, as well as an additional tape he made with reference to famous jazzman Bunk Johnson in 1954. I'd like to point out, however, that only a small portion of this vast information was used in my recent publication entitled, *Weeks Hall— The Master of the Shadows.*

The tapes include Hall's interesting experiences with his Aunt Pattee (Mrs. Walter Torian), reminiscences of his childhood, area history, the origin of south Louisiana food and the art of cooking, the early theatre, and numerous amusing stories told in his uniquely elegant manner. A more complete picture of Hall is provided in my biography. It will answer a lot of questions and make this transcribed account more exciting and meaningful.

I wish to take this opportunity to thank members of my family for the essential contributions: my wife, Helen, for her devoted counseling; my daughter, Rose Anne, for the painstaking job of correcting the transcribed account and retyping the manuscript; and my son, John, for compiling the index.

Special thanks also go out to my dear friends Diane Moore and Dr. Victoria Sullivan for their professional assistance.

I feel that the historical and delightful contents of *The Weeks Hall Tapes* will be enjoyed by both young and old, especially the inhabitants of south Louisiana. I hope you like it.

TAPE 1
(Undated)

Let it be admitted at once that I am neither a writer nor a cook, but that I do know what is set before me on the table. I know also, very well, that to the practicing cook, an introduction to a series of formulas for cooking is of as little matter as the wrapping paper in which her materials come to her. She would, at once and rightly, go to the heart of the matter at the latter part of this book and agree or disagree to that part of its contents. All good cooks are either on the defensive or the offensive. There can be no dull neutrality. The French have said, "Qui s'excuse, s'accuse."[1] If, therefore, you find these words a little on the defensive side, I hope that it will be understood that it is by way of armour and not of apology.

To show that you can never tell from whence the attack may come, I once said that "Grillades"[2] was a Louisiana parish dish. This statement was pounced upon and immediate disagreement followed. Of course, my worthy critic found it on home tables in New Orleans, but I countered her statement by defying her, and defined this dish printed upon the bills of fare of even the best public

---

[1]An old French expression which means, "He who excuses himself, accuses himself."

[2]Grillades was one of Hall's favorite dishes which consisted of lean slices of meat which were marinated, seasoned, placed in layers, browned, and served with a brown gravy.

restaurants. My statement was most generally true. But this did not prevent the probing steel point from trying to find the flaws in my armour, which I did not even imagine that I needed.

Then, there is always the eternal question of which is the original or the right receipt.[3] The discovery of the principle of the wheel is lost in obscurity, and thus it is so with receipts. The principle of the wheel has infinite applications and variations, and the ways of cookery follow this same scheme of things. All this is also true of what cooks call the right receipt. The right receipt is what the cook likes and what she likes to cook. There is no use whatever in differing with her. You simply take the receipt, which she will probably give you in some altered form, and add it or not add it to your collection. My aunt [4] told me that she had five variations of the receipt for "Les Oreilles de Cochon,"[5] which is very, very simple pastry. She kept all five receipts on paper, but only used one on the stove.

Then too, you will find in the household which is both proud and jealous of its cooking, there may occur certain postprandial discussions regarding proper credit. The family receipts could not have been used by the cook unless they had been given to her by the mistress. On the other hand, the cook will solidly and earthily maintain that the receipts were nothing but paper until they had been properly transmuted into food by her art. This old argument, without end, of which came first, the chicken or the egg, is always an endless bore. However, as I used to hear it in my aunt's

---

[3]Hall used the word receipt to mean recipe—which is correct although not commonly used.

[4]His aunt was Mrs. Walter Torian, nee Harriet Weeks, the sister of his mother Lily.

[5]"Les Oreilles de Cochon" is French for "Pigs' Ears" which the pastry resembles.

house, in relation to food, it was never such. This behind-the-scenes controversy did not occur often, but when it did it was conducted between two individuals of spirit, as would become the artists in their different roles in the drama.

TAPE 2
(April 21, 1953)

In actuality, there are a good many factors as well as personalities which enter into the complexities of a successful dinner which was made to seem so casual. These conditions are not unlike those which confront a great symphony orchestra. I have heard from professional musicians that there is an immense amount of undiscernable work which has to be brought to bear to produce a perfectly smooth performance that the audience finally hears. At her dinners, the mistress of the house is in the position of an unseen orchestra conductor. That conductor neither composes the music nor does he play the sound. He interprets. Good traditional music is like good traditional cookery. The tradition is inherently repetitious. It can only be said to be so when it is insensitively conceived. Even so, I remember Richard Strauss's reading of his *Salome* as being totally different from that of another very great conductor. You re-hear Mozart's gay G minor every time that you can, and you re-read *Huckleberry Finn* every year or two. You never tire of good, sound things.

It's tiresome to strain an analogy, but let me add another factor in which the mistress of her table has a very great advantage over those who must perform and interpret music before the general public. She can and should present her food only to those who can thoroughly appreciate its values and who are congenial among themselves. We can all join a ranch hand with his bacon and eggs, the aroma of

4

which is more than delectable. But I doubt that the ranch hand would join us in such a thing as a "daube glacé."[6]

My aunt, of whom I have spoken and of whom I shall speak much more, was blind and old and could very rarely give dinners. For these dinners, she chose from her well-guarded receipts, two or three separate selections for each dinner, with such minor seasonal variations as the receipt required. The cook thus became accustomed to doing these dishes to perfection. Things always began with a turtle soup or a gumbo and always ended with either frozen cream cheese or blackberry sherbet. Now my aunt had the kind of grand manner which is in no way assumed, but which came from wisdom and complete conviction. In my callowness, I would sometimes attempt suggestions. This always ended in my going into a corner and licking my wounds. She would say that she knew the people whom she would ask very well. She knew what these people would like. She knew that they expected certain things, and if she did not have them, they would very plainly ask her if she were going to have them. This delighted her and I think she was right.

---

[6]A glazed meat dish.

TAPE 3
(Undated)

This is not a book on gastronomy. This is a cookbook and therefore a reference book. I feel that it will be entirely fitting and sometimes diverting to give the background from which these formulas sprang—the places, the providence and the personalities.

I inherited a great many of these receipts in this collection from my aunt, who had in turn inherited them from her forebears. During the later part of her life, my aunt, a Mrs. Torian, was a childless widow, the only sister of my mother[7] of whom I am an only son. Both of these sisters were born in the room in which I write. The room is in the house which was built by my great-grandfather and great-grandmother[8] 125 years ago.

The name of the place is "The Shadows."[9] It is in the very center of the town of New Iberia, about a hundred miles directly west of New Orleans, and not very far from the Gulf, in south Louisiana. The house is fortunately intact, but the vast scattered acreages and plantations which once belonged to it have shrunk to the two acres of gardens which

---

[7]Mrs. Walter Torian was the only sister of Mrs. Mary Lily Weeks Hall.

[8]Early settler David Weeks and wife, Mary Clara Conrad Weeks.

[9]The Shadows-on-the-Teche which was bequeathed by Hall to the National Trust for Historic Preservation.

now immediately surround the house. The house was the heart of these plantations and was built directly on the banks of the Bayou Teche because the stream was navigable and it allowed uninterrupted communication with New Orleans in those days, when the roads were sometimes completely impassable. I am told that my great-grandmother gave her children property or plantations as wedding presents, in the same way George Washington gave Nellie Custis and her husband "Woodlawn" plantation, on Mount Vernon estate, as a wedding gift. My great-grandmother's brother[10] married their daughter, who is buried at Mount Vernon.

Several miles southeast of here is an upland wooded island surrounded by swamps and tidal marsh. It was known as Grand Cote, and is now known as Weeks Island. There are royal Spanish grants to him[11] from Governor Miro and Baron De Carondelet, the last Spanish Governor. On its south side, this island had access to salt water and the Gulf through deep natural bayous. Its high terrain prevented seasonal overflow before the days of levees.

From its well-drained acres later came the sugarcane and sugar which was shipped north, on schooners, and was the main support of the family. From its swamps may have come the cypress which was deadened on its roots and later used in the construction of this house, the outside shutters of which are still sound and in use after more than a century. From its marshes and its swamps, and its woods and also from its fresh water and salt water were to come the abundance of game and fish which not only appeared on the tables of its owners, but must have been part of the daily

---

[10]Charles Magill Conrad, prominent southern statesman, married Angela Lewis, the granddaughter of Fielding Lewis and Elizabeth Washington, the sister of President George Washington.

[11]William Weeks, David Weeks' father.

affairs of its tenants as well. Aside from the raising of your own domestic animals and the cultivation of your own vegetable garden, food in this milder climate was to be had merely for the going out and getting it. The cost of it all was negligible.

TAPE 4
(April 23, 1953)

There is a memento in this house which still remains as a relic, the lone and intimate connection between it and this island plantation. My grandfather and my grandmother[12] were married in 1848 and they were rowed out to Weeks Island for their honeymoon. I have my grandfather's wedding vest, a white silk damask, the pattern of which is shot with tiny threads of tarnished silver, and its buttons, covered with the same material. In this collection also are many dresses of the period. There is a dull rose taffeta evening dress and there is also what must have been a riding habit of very dark maroon velvet with a skirt of incredible length. There are laces and a shawl with French black Chantilly. There was a pair of ivory satin shoes which my mother once wore to some fancy dress party at a Virginia resort dressed as Marguerite.[13] They are laced up the side and ornamented with daisies. These are size one, mind you, and their soles show evidence of having been used only once.

In one of the upper rooms here, there is a portrait of my mother as a girl, painted in the 1850's in the same room in which it now hangs. It was done in pastel, and shows no evidences, after almost a century, of the mildew which

---

[12]William F. Weeks and Mary Palfrey Weeks.

[13]Marguerite is a species of daisy.

9

usually attacks pictures, done in this medium, in this very humid climate.

In this same room there also hangs, framed under glass, the dress which she wore when this portrait was done so long ago. Among other portraits on these walls here, there is one of my grandfather's sister,[14] who was lost to the great tropical hurricane which struck Last Island[15] in the middle of the last century. She was never seen again. The bodies of her children were found and they are buried in cast-iron coffins molded in cast-iron drapery and lie beside my great-grandmother in the family burial place on the grounds here.

Last Island was a long narrow strip of sand with small trees but a very few feet above sea level and completely isolated from the mainland by many miles of impassable marsh. This place at that time was a great resort for plantation owners and their families. In those days of no storm warnings, the hurricane struck very suddenly and the waters met over the low island and destroyed everything. Lafcadio Hearn, in his *Chita*, uses this very hurricane on Last Island as a basis for his story. These storms are frequent here and my mother used to describe them as they passed over the old, long, low wooden house[16] on the hill at Weeks Island, which must have been built there at about the same time that this one was. She used to say that the house there would rock in the intermittent gusts of wind, then settle down between them like an old setting hen.

---

[14]Frances Weeks Magill Prewitt.

[15]Last Island, also known as Isle Derniere, is located in the Gulf of Mexico, south of Houma, La.

[16]House no longer exists.

TAPE 5

(April 26, 1953)

My father[17] came from New York to practice law before the Civil War and became a Confederate major. I am told that my grandfather here was known never to even utter the least audible of rebel yells. I never knew him because he died at about the time that I was born. But in my childhood I had heard many stories about him. He was evidently a very simple man of vast amiability and a keen and overpowering sense of the ridiculous toward himself and toward other men.

I had inherited his great and elephantine dining table[18] with its possible extension of nine leaves. It was being moved out to be replaced by another smaller and more suitable one. The family doctor had dropped in that day to have coffee with me. He became silent at the sight of this removal and the many memories which it brought back to him. But he recovered his professional composure long enough to remark to me that this table had killed more people in Iberia Parish from over-eating than any other.

In my grandmother's day, great tureens of gumbo, with its accompanying dishes of rice, were placed before her at the

---

[17]Gilbert Lewis Hall.

[18]Hall gave the table to his friend Archie Campbell.

11

foot of the table. When all of the soup plates were filled, and as the meal progressed, my grandfather would go on with the gumbo until he had exhausted what was in his plate, and then send it down to the other end of the table to his wife, saying that he had eaten the gumbo. When the plate had been filled and sent back to him, he started in on the rice. When this was gone, he would send back the plate and say, "Mary, I shall like to have more rice." This ordinary procedure was repeated with all gravity as a matter of custom until he had had his fill.

Of course, all of this led to a diet. He'd follow it scrupulously and truthfully tell his doctor that he had done so. But of course, any diet for him would mean about as much as a couple of cocktail canapes would mean today. He thought of any diet, however lenicnt, as nothing but a pill to be taken before his regular meal. It was not a substitute at all, but merely a tuning up before the real business began. And so it was with the small and separate oval dishes of different foods which were placed before him in restaurants.

TAPE 6
(Undated)

He maintained that these were only samples and he ordered more from the small dishes of that which he liked. These were the days of enormous breakfasts, and I believe that the very many different hot breads of corn and of wheat, of which we have the receipts, played their role at this morning meal. The descriptions of other main dishes now seem preposterous. Of course, the conditions of the life were different. There was more leisure for the meal, and there was less artificial physical confinement afterward. Under such circumstances, especially in the country, the body needed such fuel to fortify itself against the immediate and prolonged activities which followed.

Long before the substantial family breakfasts at the table, there occurred a rite which is peculiar to south Louisiana. This was the early morning coffee, which is brought to the bedroom shortly after the break of day. This coffee was, as they say, purest of virgins, black as the devil, and hot as hell. Even the children had theirs at this time, in the form of a weak "cafe au lait."

The men of the family had theirs even before this, perhaps in the kitchen, while it was being made. In the black hours of the morning, if the men were going hunting or fishing, they and their attendants would always contrive to line their stomachs with this scalding brew. This minor opening theme of black coffee continues throughout each day and pervades and underlies the life of the people of this whole region. Its offer is never omitted in either business or social contact, and you will find it before you, whether in the heavy china of the cabins or in the silver pots of the planter. The serving of tea is almost unknown here. Instead, the women have what they call coffee parties. With the usual kind of tea food, this is always done immediately before the lunch hour. Perhaps its mild stimulation is needed in a warm and somewhat debilitating climate.

TAPE 7
(April 27, 1953)

During the first half of the last century, the land was cheap and the plantation houses, their dependencies and their quarters, together with their sugar mills, were surrounded by immense tracts of land, fields under cultivation, primeval forests, and swamps of cypress. Thus, there were great distances between these houses and they were separated by roads which at best were only rough in dry weather and impassable in wet. Our communication was to be had by such natural bayous as already existed and which the lay of the land allowed. Each plantation was a community in itself, and was self-supporting.

Very little food came in from the outside, and the cost of it came not from the buying of it, but from the labor and the hazards of raising it. The receipts of each plantation, therefore, were the result of what you had raised yourself.

The great distances between these islands of people, surrounded by their necessities and luxuries, allowed of no casual visit. You went to these houses with a foreknowledge of a long and arduous journey, but you went to them also with the assurance that you and everyone whom you brought with you were to receive the generous hospitality of the owner for as long as you cared to stay.

This meant that you, and perhaps your family, went in your traveling carriage, and your groom, and the horses and other servants had to be housed and taken care of. This meant that the owner not only had to have ready many facilities for the housing of these frequent guests and whoever came with them, but that in some way he had to keep stored such unseasonal food as might be required. There was no going around the corner to the A&P for something; when you ran out of it, you simply ran out. On one hand, there was no thermostatic control of heating, and on the other, there was not the magic convenience of a deep freeze. Yet in our present-day slick paper advertisements, those days were called the days of gracious living.

I suppose that the application with that term depended upon which end you found yourself. It is said that Thomas Jefferson discovered that other people found him so gracious that he had periodically to move out. Despite this, he died in debt. He retired from public life internationally famous, and to his country acres came the great of both continents. Also, his country seat was just far enough from Washington to be a convenient stopping-over place for those going north or south for reasons of necessity or pleasure. He was a man of resource and I imagine that he easily faded out when the peak loads would come. And at those times, in very practical self-defense, he simply had to leave.

The families were very large and it followed that there were a great many cousins, either by marriage or by birth. Among these was always to be found the type which was on the receiving or gracious end, and who always made the rounds, visiting in turn the various plantations. By no means in this category was a cousin who came here from a Bayou LaFourche plantation to stay for a month, I believe in the 1880's. He died here in 1906, a very gentle old man, who is part of all of us. I was never allowed in his room, because he kept in an armoire there all sorts of hand-reloading material for shotgun shells and large red canisters of gun powder, which was probably too stale to go off anyway.

TAPE 8
(April 28, 1953)

My mother used to tell an amusing story about this man's father who was one of the few doctors along the LaFourche in those days. It seems that the doctor had been challenged to a duel by a man who used the pretext that the doctor had been peeping at this man's wife while she was taking her bath. The doctor was known as an excellent marksman and he tried in every reasonable way to avoid this encounter. It could not be done, and seconds were appointed and everything arranged. The doctor's opponent chose the sideways firing position, presenting a narrower target, as is described in Sheridan's play, *The Rivals.*[19] The doctor came out unscathed, but he shot his opponent in what my mother used to call the fleshy part of the hip. He immediately handed his own second his pistol, with the suggestion that this second tell his opponent's second that as a doctor, he was at their service to probe for and remove the ball with the prepared surgical instruments that always accompanied the pistols to a duel. His choleric opponent replied that he had put it there, and, damn it, he was going to leave it there.

Of the two sisters here, my mother was the elder. My mother was born in 1851, but my aunt would never tell

---

[19]Richard Brinsley Sheridan wrote the comedy, "The Rivals," which was first produced at Covent Garden, London, England, on Jan. 17, 1775.

anything about her age, and would bristle at any question put to her about it. And indeed, today, at her request, the date of her birth does not appear upon the marble door of her tomb.[20] After her death, the carver of such inscriptions said that she had very pointedly told him that she would never forgive his putting it there, even in an after-life.

There was a great difference in age between the two sisters. During the first third of my aunt's life, she was what was then known as a nervous invalid. And my grandfather would regularly take a cottage at White Sulphur Springs,[21] and from there go on to Saratoga[22] and the various fashionably curative watering places, which were thought best for her condition. In the garret, I still have a great many stereoscopic views of these places and an old machine, which would show them to you by simply turning a handle. These detailed and rigid photographs shown in this machine were a fascination to me, when I was allowed to see them as some childhood reward, in the garret.

When the slates were cool on a summer, rainy day, invalids in my childhood, from the talk around me, seemed to contain nothing but calf's foot jelly and beef tea. Their importance came mainly from the time that it took to make them. I was accustomed to hear, however, that many of the hot bread receipts and the dessert receipts came from Virginia, either from staying there frequently, or from relatives there.

My grandmother, they say, always said that everybody in Virginia was related to everybody else, or if they weren't, they said they were. My languid and fragile young aunt, as she approached womanhood, was the center of all solicitation in the family. Her attacks at this time were

---

[20]Buried at Metairie Cemetery, New Orleans, La.

[21]White Sulphur Springs, West Virginia.

[22]Saratoga Springs, New York.

foreseen and prevented by the gratification of every possible desire and every wistful request. As her invalidism gradually and fortunately disappeared, she became robust. All that remained of this former condition was her lifelong and inherent air of command. She was very active during her maturity, but she again became an invalid through total blindness during the last twenty years of her life. She had a way with her, when she wished, of completely ignoring people and circumstances to the point where they did not exist at all for her. She chose at its very inception to sublimely ignore this disability and it was never even mentioned. Strangers to her did not even suspect it.

TAPE 9
(April 29, 1953)

In the long years between her first and her final affliction, my aunt was very active. In her later years, she married and became the mistress of her own house. It was at that time, I believe, that she became interested in preserving the family receipts and in the collecting of others. Even after she had moved to New Orleans to live and to become a widow, she continued to be interested mainly in adding country receipts to her collection. The city proved not an entirely infertile field for this. In times past, the older families had either periodically gone there or periodically lived there to see, and to bring back with them, all the luxuries which were not to be had in the country. Where possible, they had brought back with them too, some of the receipts of the outer and greater world with which New Orleans was then so directly connected. From the descendants of these families, my aunt got many of these receipts or variations of those which she already had. The search for them was unending and sometimes frustrating. Cooks have no professional ethics except that of secrecy. And this, after all, is only the overwhelming instinct of self-preservation. She would worm her way shamelessly into the affections of anyone who possessed a unique receipt. I remember a double victory, when she got from two branches one of the family receipts which neither branch would give the other. It was a great sport and she gloried in it. All good cooks do.

Very long before all this, my aunt had emerged from the

earlier wan phase of invalidism into the fresher and more invigorating air of the 90's. However fresh and invigorating that air may have been, I remember from my earliest childhood that the pink and ruffled chest in her room always supported an enormous variety of bottles and jars of creams and lotions and perfumes and good-smelling things to a child. Pink and white complexions meant everything, and when she set forth for the throw line for redfish in the deep waters of Weeks Bayou below the island, she went swathed in veils and gloves as the earlier motorists used to do. My grandfather was a great trotting horse enthusiast, and he gave her a pair of matched black ponies. He had a white canvas harness made for them, and here she drove them tandem with a large pink bow on the buggy whip, up and down the main street.

It was a most fortunate coincidence that radio came into common use at just about the time that she became blind. I would give her the best of these instruments as they came out every year or two. As her pride and her infirmity prevented her moving from her large chair, she became an absorbed listener and fumbled for the dial all day long to get what programs she wanted. She could tell you in advance what programs came on at what hour and on what days. She would have people write the high officials of each broadcasting system and tell them of what programs she disapproved and why. Thus, she continued her devotion to this branch of the theatre, music, throughout her sightless days.

She was also the only one whom I've ever known to contrive to use this machine as a weapon of self-defense. When some insufferable bore, and insufferable bores always come bearing the seeds of their destruction within them, would chatter on, she would casually, as though there were no one in the room, lean to her right and turn the radio at full volume. The resulting crash would startle and unnerve this species of visitor. The thunder of all this would fill the room and go on until such a time as my aunt deemed it proper to stop it. She would then very sweetly ask, "What were you saying, my dear?" and repeat these doses as she thought them necessary.

TAPE 10
(Undated)

It was rather a relief to me when the radio came to her and when she did not have to go to the theatre. She'd long been a lover of the theatre, and on her visit to New York, spent much time in its audiences. She had the names of all the casts at her fingertips, and reserved seats far in advance. It might be mentioned that here, in this small town[23] at the turn of the century, there appeared such plays as *Diplomacy* and *Candida* for one-night stands with their New York casts. In her later years, she would accept no seat but that on the front row in the middle in the center section. This may have been all right for her, as she was deaf in one ear, but it was very hard on those who went with her. If you happened to get on her deaf side, she would shout conversation at you in the midst of any line going on on the stage.

I remember well her last appearance in the theatre, at least with me. She had insisted on being taken to see Ethel Barrymore[24] in some light play tailored to that star. She always went very early, which was fortunate, because she was a formidable figure to convoy to her seat. After a very long wait, the curtain went up on the usual trivial lines which would enable the audience to find their seats before the appearance of the star. She finally appeared in the

---

[23]New Iberia, La.

[24]Ethel Barrymore, famous American actress (1879-1959).

doorway of backstage center. There was tremendous and prolonged applause, followed by a breathless silence awaiting the rich loveliness of that great voice. My aunt turned and yelled at me, "Has she dyed her hair?" I knew then that I had seated myself on her deaf side. Well, Miss Barrymore's profile has always been a line of the sheerest beauty. I try to remember this but, that night, at that moment, I could see nothing but the enormous Barrymore eyes. They filled the whole proscenium. Being a thoroughbred, she probably ran through the rest of the play on batteries, as I call it. I remember nothing, whatever, of the rest of the evening.

In the prime days of the legitimate stage, my aunt would think nothing of going to New Orleans to see a great performance, just as the Creoles were accustomed to going from their plantations to hear the opera. When New York sent out minor players in the leading roles and inadequate casts, the theatre in the provinces died. It was supplanted somehow by the movies, for which she never cared.

Later, in New Orleans, when she lived alone, and when her infirmities had not reached the stage where she could not go out by herself, she went regularly to vaudeville and the variety shows. On Wednesday nights, she always had the same memorable front-row center seat. She cared little for the varied miscellaneous bill of acts which preceded the appearance of the headliner of that week. If these players were unknown to her, she would give the tickets away. She now regularly bought *Billboard* and *Variety* to see in advance what was coming out of New York. This may all seem pathetic, but remember that the headliners were very frequently the great performers of her youth, and these were their last performances.

I remember in Philadelphia once going to see Lillie Langtry[25] under the same circumstances, merely because my

_____

[25]Lillie or Lilly Langtry (1853-1929) was a famous British actress who was publicized as being one of the most beautiful woman of her time.

24

mother had frequently spoken of her as being a great beauty in her day. I like to think that my aunt sat through such things as Fink's mules and Chinese fire-eaters merely because she wanted to pay her final respects to the great figures in the art of the theatre who are bygones today.

TAPE 11
(April 30, 1953)

The old house here was vacant, except for a caretaker, for a long time during my formative years. My mother first lived in New Orleans and then in North Carolina for her health. After marrying, my aunt lived in her own house in a small town near here,[26] and afterwards, she and her husband went to New Orleans to live.[27] I lived in New Orleans first, then went to Philadelphia to school,[28] and from there, I went abroad on traveling scholarships. In all this time, I remember only once coming back to this empty and desolate place. The grounds were overgrown and the separate kitchen and quarters of brick had fallen into ruin, as well as had the two small glass hothouses.

The house itself was almost as structurally sound as it is today, but it was separated and shuttered seemingly against all time. The things inside were left just as they were many years before. They were all in their familiar places, and for the moment you seem never to have left them. Under their veils of dust, these inanimate but well-remembered things seemed silently to call out to be touched and used again. In one dim room, there were the same four family portraits of

---

[26]Lafayette, Louisiana.

[27]2624 South Carrollton Avenue.

[28]Pennsylvania Academy of Fine Arts.

the forties, of identical size, and in identical old gilt frames. On one of these were perched a pair. . .[29] (the tape is damaged here).

They didn't screech. These things don't screech, they mourn, almost inaudibly. When they do cry, too repeatedly, too near to your house at night, you may silence them, as they say, by getting up and turning a sock wrong-side out and putting it near the fireplace. After this visit, I didn't come back to the place for a long time,[30] and when I did, it was to repair it, to paint it, to make it more comfortable, and to live here as I do now.

And the old kitchen[31] here was, as is customary with such buildings on plantations in the old South, apart from the house and about 50 feet away on the Bayou Teche side. It was of brick and paved brick and was peculiar in that it had a brick chimney running free through the roof in the exact center. In this chimney were two great fireplaces on either side so that cooking could be done simultaneously in both fireplaces. These separate outside kitchens were said to prevent the odors of cooking from coming into the main house. I believe, however, that, as these homes were usually symmetrical, they had no place for the larger fireplaces which the space for cooking required. I have still preserved, downstairs, the scarred old, cypress kitchen table.[32] The top consists of two planks, each about two feet across and about seven or eight feet long. Think of these dimensions as applied to a modern apartment kitchenette. The pantry, brick paved, was, however, with sensible forethought placed in a room within the walls of the big house.

---

[29]Hall was probably referring to owls. Owls still roost near the house.

[30]May, 1922.

[31]The kitchen was torn down.

[32]The table is still at the Shadows.

TAPE 12
(May 1, 1953)

(I cannot any longer even try to be consecutive with these paragraphs. Many years ago, I found a book of collected essays. I have never been able to find it since, nor do I know the names. Lafcadio Hearn has an essay in this book on literary composition. Someone had asked him whether you began to write and just finished as you went along until you came to the end. To this, he says, "By no means. You write down what occurs to you, and if the thing which occurs to you is intense enough, it will grow, as you may put it, from either end, and they will eventually connect themselves when they are rearranged, or you can connect them by the beginning or the end of each paragraph or by a paragraph in between."

I'm not a writer, and with this tape I have no other resource from now on than to simply put down these paragraphs, and when they are typed, each to a separate page, rearrange them until they are satisfactory, after being proofread, punctuated and dependent clauses put in the right place and so on. Forgive me if I have to do this.)

The house now rests, surrounded by great live oaks which were planted by the builders, in the middle of a whole block in the center of the town which has grown up around it.

It was the custom in the old days for many plantation owners to have the burial grounds of their family not far from the house on their own property. Such was the case here, and my great- grandmother, Mary Conrad Weeks, is buried between two magnolia trees in the corner of the grounds.

During the Civil War, the Union General Banks[33] had his headquarters in the room immediately beneath the room in which I write. He and his staff did everything that they could for the mistress of the house which sheltered them both. She would have none of it. Instead, she moved to a room in the garret on the third floor, and there, in willful seclusion and stringent circumstances, she died and was immediately buried in the corner of the grounds here, in the family plot. Her grave, now in dense shade and covered with ivy, lies not far, on her right, from the roar of traffic of a great transcontinental highway. And near the head of her grave, this main artery is intersected by Weeks Street, immediately beyond which is the dense tumult of the business section of the town. This plot and all of the property is surrounded by a concealing and high bamboo hedge, from the outside of which even the house is scarcely visible now.

All is usually very quiet here, within the precincts of the property, and a bamboo hedge, especially on the bayou side, does much to protect you from what lies outside it. I once had the high privilege and pleasure of having had the General Ulysses S. Grant III here. I have never had a more graciously interested visitor. I took him all over the house and the grounds here, and told him as much of the history of the place as I could. We had got to the latticed summer house overlooking the bayou, and nothing could have been more peaceful. Suddenly, all conversation was drowned beneath a great whirring noise. It filled the air. The repair shop next door across the street had chosen that moment to sand the paint from automobile bodies. When it stopped, the General could not help but ask what it was. I told him, of course, but I think that I added to someone else in the party that it may have been my great-grandmother turning over in her grave.

_____

[33] Major General Nathaniel Banks.

TAPE 13
(May 3, 1953)

There appears to be no comparable section of our whole country in which good regional cookery plays such a large part. Even in this state, the area seems to be confined to a wider or narrower strip close to the Gulf of Mexico. This may partly be due to an extremely rich alluvial deposit, as well as the enormous stretches of water here, which merge imperceptibly into the salt waters of the Gulf. The love of cooking here may also be attributed to an inheritance from our Gaelic traditions. It seems to be found in neither of the states along the Gulf immediately adjoining us. Cooking here surpasses even the necessity of the housewife cooking for her man and her family. Independently of all this, the producing of it has become the aim and object of certain connoisseurs among men, just as chamber music used to be played by people who were not professionals, merely for the joy of playing it. The custom of which I shall speak has largely gone out of existence, but the fond gastronomic memories of it still remain.

It was a men-only affair, at least as far as the kitchen and the table were concerned. The women were allowed to wash the dishes. The need for this feast arose spontaneously and intermittently among men who liked to cook and whose cooking was very well known, and who would have as their companions only gourmets with the same stripe.

These suppers were given in anyone's house, but I well remember one of them at which I was a guest in my own house of one of this very limited group of cooks. There were a tractor salesman, a doctor, a bootlegger, an attorney and a farmer. The cook on this occasion was a mechanic in a public garage. He had a great reputation and he was as expansive in temperament as well as in his proportions. He arrived first with his materials, which had come as gifts from the various guests. He placed his bottle of corn whiskey on the window sill, next to the stove, and also a small bottle of caramel, which is sugar, burned and diluted, and goes in almost last. As the expected men straggled into the kitchen, he put them to work preparing the various ingredients. Don't worry, they had come to watch. As the catfish was being boiled and its bones removed, he started his roux. As its smoothness came, through interminable stirring, and as its aroma became more and more mouthwatering, the contents of the corn liquor bottle decreased. In town here, he had chosen French bread in lieu of rice, which is always available in faraway places when bread is not.

There was discussion in the kitchen, then with one accord, compliments burst forth from one end of the table to the other. When he deemed it finished, it was brought in soup plates into the dining room with bottles of beer. Now, incredibly, each of these seated men could have told the courtbouillon[34] made by one man from the courtbouillon made by another. Otherwise they would not have been there.

---

[34] A highly-seasoned fish broth served with rice.

TAPE 14
(Undated)

Before attacking the steaming dish, there was, on the part of each, a restrained (and restrained is the word) silence. This silence even continued after the first few spoonfuls, so that each individual palate might savour and weigh the final result of such long preparation. Then they simultaneously burst forth, from all around the table, the justified compliments. This is a matter of course and of the traditional French politesse. Even after this, there was not much talking among these men, until the bottom of this first soup plate appeared.

At about this time, they would begin to discuss, with the cook, the present courtbouillon and former ones from his hands. This would be followed by a round table about the courtbouillons of other people, and then each man would go into details of the making of his own courtbouillon. The variations were always very minor—of time and ingredients. These discussions were always amiable and even enthusiastic. But one can never know the amount of mental reservation which was brought there. These comparisons of opinions always struck me as being comparable only to discussions on the reading of the same piece of music by different musicians. You have to know your music.

Occasionally, a cook has to make certain individual compensations in his receipt for some reason best known to himself. Years ago, the first cellist of a great symphony orchestra once told me that after a violin concerto, he had timidly asked the soloist why he had interpolated certain notes which were not in the original score by the composer. The soloist casually and simply replied that he was a violinist, and had not realized certain purely physical obstacles which stood in the way of a smooth rendition. It was necessary for the soloist, perhaps because of his individual style, to either add or take away a few notes in order to get full intention of the music.

So it is with cooks. As an amusing instance, so it was with my aunt's lifelong and open warfare against the use of ham, in whatever small quantity, as an ingredient in gumbo. This smoldered, until at last she came upon a printed receipt for gumbo containing ham, which appeared in a national magazine of the widest circulation. Over this she yowled and sputtered for days, almost to the point where she would have written the editors of the magazine and the Postmaster General—the magazine contained unprintable stuff. I never dared tell her, one of the best gumbos I ever had in my life was made from the carcasses of wild duck and contained . . . ham!

TAPE 15
(May 3, 1953)

In connection with cooking, when we speak of the traditional Gaelic influences here, we must speak of the origins of the people who enabled it to survive. There are two distinct kinds of cuisine. New Orleans was settled by a richer and freer class of the French, who brought cosmopolitanism to the young metropolis, which not only received trade from the fresh water bottoms, which floated down the Mississippi, but which also exported and imported many diverse things by way of the salt waters of the Gulf of Mexico.

They became very rich, but later, after the invention of the granulation of sugar by Etienne de Boré, they secured their finances by the acquisition of large acreages of land. These plantations were either on, or very near, every possible navigable stream for the convenience and the necessity of transportation in those days. This class continued to live much as they did in France. They had a large house in the city and another one in the country, when they did not go abroad.

In the history of North America, there were the French who had settled in eastern Canada. Most eastern of all these provinces was a peninsula jutting out into the north Atlantic on most of the sides. Nova Scotia is entirely agricultural, earning its hard northern living from its fields and from the sea. It was isolated and undefended and, by the circumstances of its position, was a prime target for the

British navy during the French and Indian wars. They landed, attacked, pillaged, and captured most of the peaceable natives of the region called Acadia. With their homes and everything which they possessed in the hands of the enemy, they either found or sought refuge on the coast of Louisiana. Except for the milder climate, they found their occupations much the same as those they had left. They found land which by hard work could be made tillable, and they found that that land was not far from the sea, to which they were so much accustomed. They stayed and they are here now. The names which we find here today are exactly the names which exist in Nova Scotia today. The Creoles of New Orleans are emigrés. The Acadians here, in mid-south Louisiana, were refugees. One class was mainly urban, the other class was entirely rural. These latter people were, and are, called "Acadians." The word "cajun" is not a corruption, but a contraction for the word "Acadian." Repeat the original word rapidly to yourself and you can easily see how, in the rapidity of ordinary speech, such a contraction naturally came about.

It is a noble survival today, among a once-bitterly oppressed people, that their place of origin in the new world so many years ago should be so instinctively remembered. Between New Orleans and our region lies a wide, dense and impenetrable strip of marsh and swamp. In the former years of lack of individual transportation, this geographic barrier[35] separated the two groups. But to the French mind, which combines a sense of sound tradition and of sound realities, they were never separated. They relish life to the utmost and this is what we call our Gaelic inheritance.

---

[35]Meaning the Atchafalaya Basin.

TAPE 16
(May 4, 1953)

Those who came to the shores of the New America to live brought with them the formulas for cooking to which they were accustomed in the land which they had left. Due to inevitable differences in climate, terrain, and waters, they could not always exactly duplicate the results of these receipts. However, they approximated these results by substituting, as far as possible, the indigenous products of their new environment. Sometimes, they found the Indian dishes, made from entirely indigenous materials, were to their liking. These they refined and used as a supplement to their accustomed European fare. This was particularly true of Indian maize. The Spanish dominations contributed to the high seasoning which certain palates found welcome. When the Africans were brought in from their strips along the west coast, into our warmer latitudes, to which they were not unaccustomed, they too brought in their native foods. And they, like the others, found adaptations necessary for the reason that in their new world they could not find the things which they had used at home.

There is a strange connection to this sort of thing which an old friend once told me. She was a New Orleans woman whose house and whose food were always perfect. She brought over her own French cook, whose husband was the apple-cheeked chauffeur of a high Renault town car. She summered in France and had many connections there.

This enabled her, during the First World War, to get the

French government to allow her to endow a small wing of a war hospital and to go abroad to serve as best she could with it. In this wing, the French government had placed many of the native Senegalese war wounded. We all seem very far away from home in hospitals and these poor people were very far from home, in fact. There was little in France to give at that time. The people would occasionally bring in their common garden flowers or wild flowers in season. She told me that she could never forget the sight of the long, slender and almost delicate hands of these patients as they looked and looked into these blossoms.

Now hospital food is very good for you, but it is not very good. Somehow, it is all colorless and white. Out of curiosity and sympathy, she commenced to ask some of the reviving and convalescent patients about what kind of food they had at home. After getting on the right side of the diet experts and with the amiable cooperation of whatever native cooks they may have had, she approximated a gumbo. I don't know what kind, but they did. It was home cooking to a soldier and though home cooking to every soldier is different, it is always the same. She saw that in their faces.

TAPE 17
(May 5, 1953)

(I have found that it is absolutely impossible to make these paragraphs or this matter consecutive. These are rough drafts—rough on the recorder and probably still more rough on the listener.)

On evening, in Paris, many years ago, a friend of mine told me that he had been taken that afternoon to meet Marcel Cachin, the great French radical. He told me that his gnarled old fingers which had once thrown bombs, were now occupied with embroidery as he sat quietly in his chair. He also told me that this old fighter had, in the mildest manner, asked him endless and penetrating questions about the gigantic and palatial hotels of New York. The bigger and more intricate was their organization, the more he was interested. He wanted to know how the management could direct the details of everything in such a tremendous undertaking. He was interested most of all in the great hotel kitchens. He wanted to know how their raw materials for cooking reached them and if these supplies came from sources controlled by themselves. He wanted to know how the dishes on the daily bills of fare were decided upon so that they would be most satisfactory to the people who were to have them ... (defect in tape)

The old man knew that hundreds of thousands of people under one roof, sometimes a block square, was a perfectly practical matter. It had existed for years in apartment houses. But he also seemed to think that the running of individual households and the time consumed in preparing individual dishes in each separate kitchen was a waste of time. Hotel life is a communal life and that was his thread of connection. It made no difference to him that at the great and expensive hotels the various individual services to the various individual guests was the highest point of their efficiency, and possibly the very reason for their existence. Each room in the vast building can be made so comparatively alike that they will satisfy every reasonable condition for comfortable living. You can't do this with stomachs, nor with appetites. Every housewife awakens with this problem every morning. It was a royallist, and not a revolutionary, who found out long before that you cannot even let them eat cake regularly.

When you are a child in the country, every clear breaking summer day is the creation of the world. Yesterday had not existed. On such days, very early in the morning, after I had had my coffee milk, as they call it here, I would occasionally go to the market with my father and I was allowed to carry the empty basket. My father used to wear what seemed to be, by common consent, a uniform—a black alpaca coat and Calcutta-seersucker trousers which swished as he walked. His collars and his cuffs, separate from his shirt, were stiff as segments of armour. The bow ties were the wonder of it all. They came packed as carefully as an orchid, six to a box, white and immaculate, of some sheer material which is pressed into a flat bow with not even hems to break their rigidity. With a broad-brimmed Panama hat and an umbrella, this was the dress of the older, professional men in their offices or upon the streets in the small town or in New Orleans.

TAPE 18
(Undated)

I was allowed to carry the empty basket up. But on what seemed then the very long walk back, I sometimes shared the load with my elderly father. No matter who went for the marketing, the basket was always heavy. It bore not only the needs of the immediate family, but of the cook and those who worked here as well. It was perfectly understood, and taken for granted, that you [36] took home to her own family in her own basket such part of this as they needed or wanted, and this was provided. Some foods they would not eat at all, for instance, the lamb or mutton. Barring the great American fortunes in the east, the gap at the turn of the century here between the well-to-do and their servants was little above that which existed immediately after the Civil War. The gap has lessened incalculably due to the higher wages paid by industry.

The running of the home is not made for profit. Nor can the householder increase the principal and pass it on to the employees as the industrialists frequently must do. It is only reasonable that families follow better living conditions and better living conditions are brought about by more pay for the head of the family. This releases the untrained women from drudgery and the children for school. It is a long-term investment, but every rational mind knows that it will eventually pay off. But every sentimental and luxurious mind cannot help but deplore it. After all, the servantless

---

[36] Weeks Hall was referring to the cook and servants.

house in the North, in the hands of the thrifty, has existed for years. Thrift has never been any part of the South, due perhaps to its well-known absence from any warmer climate and the tradition of deputizing work.

There are a few cooks who are given to saving money for other people. Not many regularly-employed cooks of any kind are left. They and their families have followed their menfolk to urban and industrial centers. They have found there, not only higher pay, but the choice of more manifold opportunities, as well as for the promise of their children more varied occupations in which to be trained. In agricultural areas, such as here, they are freed from the seasonal hazards of the fields. There are only two or three months of regular sugar-making activity, and if a freeze should occur, even that is blotted out. The good old days, as sentimentalists call them, are gone. In their place, we have rapid transportation, preservation, refrigeration and complete electrification in the service part of the house. Wisely used, these not only save time and hands, but most particularly do they defy the seasons. However, all this will occasionally mean nothing to sentimentalists who hold out on either side of the pantry door.

I knew a cook who had never used an electric mixer for anything. She would mix things laboriously by hand, because she claimed that they tasted better that way. She may have been on the side of the angels after all, for very far back I remember the ceremonial making of the eggnog by my old godmother in her dining room on Christmas Eve in New Orleans. No servant had any part in the making of it, though they later shared in it with us all. It was the chiffon kind, which stands on its own feet. The old lady was surrounded by equal parts of family and her old hands whisked in a deep flat silver platter, starting at intervals to add such soul and spirit to the matter as she wished. This was handed to her by her nephews in two well-worn and well-known bottles. There were no night clubs in those days to later blot out its memory.

TAPE 19
(May 13 1953)

(This whole thing has subsided into a series of notes. For instance, what immediately follows belongs up with the matter concerning my aunt's love of the theatre.)

This was a very small town in the 1900's, but it was directly on the main line of the Southern Pacific Railway, leading directly out of New Orleans to a West which was eager for amusement, New York, or culture. Where did the audiences come from? They fell all over themselves to go to the ticket window and buy little pieces of cardboard. You did not have piped into your home electric weather, electric sounds and electric sights day after day and hour after hour.

The Vendôme Opera House was in the next block from here and to it came everything when anything came. Its curtain was the physical embodiment of anticipation. Its central panel was an empty street scene from which I am convinced Corico got all of his Coricos. This true American primitive was surrounded by what appeared to be miles of painted red plush and a frenzy of painted rococo frames, in each of which was lettered in plain black and white the current advertisement of the day: the meat market, the livery stable, and the drug store, the harness maker and the barber shop, with its hot and cold baths. It always rose with thunderous applause on the same worn and tattered sets of scenery, just as it did at the French Opera in New Orleans. The eyes of the audience were so accustomed to it that it literally did not exist. This audience reaction is both very old

42

and very new. It happened with the ancient Chinese traditional theatre, and it happens today with a constructivist interpretation of any play.

The fare, which was chosen by the usual traveling stock companies, was about on a par with the repertoire of the showboats which moored here on the bayou once a year. Occasionally, a great star would come out of New York for a tour of one night stands across the country. This gave my stage-struck young aunt ideas. The transient accomodations in the town were limited and primitive. We were a block from the theatre. The original plan of the house has an outside curved stairway leading from the lower porch to the upper and directly to the head of which was a guest room. The stairway is shuttered between the columns and gives a sort of privacy to this entrance. My aunt would, far in advance, contrive to make this room available to such stars of the legitimate stage as were then nationally known. It was also the bishop's room when he came here for confirmations, usually on Palm Sundays.

I like this combination of the bishop or the actresses, but my aunt liked much more the combination of the actresses and herself. You cannot have much to eat immediately before the work of a performance, but these women came here ravenous afterwards. They didn't have to think of their figures in those days and trays and trays of things which they had never had before would come to them as they sat relaxed before the wood fire of the bedroom. I use the word "relaxed" in a very special sense of the term, for my aunt was always there and she would put to them questions about their greater world and about themselves. As artists like to talk about themselves more than anything else, I assure you that there was no strain upon either digestion or conversation as the firewood died into embers. All the rest of the family had long before been in bed asleep.

TAPE 20
(May 10, 1953)

A house of twenty-two rooms, a gastronomic adventure in the grand manner, in New Orleans in my early teens, knocked me out.

I was going to high school and lived apart from my mother and my aunt with two old Creole ladies who never spoke to each other except in words of the highest blame. The fact that one was almost totally deaf made no difference to the other. The deaf one arose at three in the afternoon and retired at three the next morning. They had the most beautiful old things, all of which were wrapped in the spring and taken out again in the fall. There was one large room at the back of the house, half of which was barred off with brown slats and always kept locked against the other half. The wide shelves of this sanctuary held immense sets of china and glassware, each piece wrapped individually in dust-covered brown paper.

On the occasion of which I speak, the brown paper was taken off. There emerged china of the most exquisite pattern. As I remember it, it was white and gray and gold and canary yellow. The occasion was the giving of a large dinner party to a man and his wife from the North who had come to New Orleans. There was much preparation before, which started with the infinite care of the washing and handling of the old crystal and china which had not seen the light of day for years. Then there came the ordering of the food, for a certain date, but all from different dealers. After this, there was much consulting of opinion as to which dealer could furnish the most dependable shell for the "vol-au-vent."[37] I have never seen a "vol-au-vent" from that day to this, but its name has come in handy in describing certain people.

I was very young, but I was graciously asked to the table because these people were friends of my mother and because I was the only other occupant of this large house. Well, this was a long, drawn out sort of affair where sherbet comes in the middle. With me, sherbet had always come at the end, and I started to get up, until someone next to me pinched me and put me back in my place. The end, much later on, of course, was an ornamented "bisque glacé"[38] from Lopez. Usually, to be taken to Lopez on Canal Street for this delicacy was a great treat. By now, I could only look at it.

This long parade of "haute cuisine"[39] bewildered me. And what I do remember most vividly of it had nothing to do with the superiority of the dishes. The guest of honor was a very tall man, white-haired and direct. His opposite number, who had been asked especially to meet him, was a Creole of distinguished lineage, short and squat and bow-legged and bald. The rest of the table went about their affairs, but the tall man, finding himself in good voice, droned on throughout the whole dinner with the larynx of an Elmer Davis.[40] He was stopped, but momentarily, by the high odor of the game course when it assailed his northern

---

[37]A large, light patty shell.

[38]Usually means a chilled, thick, creamy soup. But here Hall probably meant a chilled dessert.

[39]High-style cooking.

[40]Elmer Davis (1890-1958). Well-known American newspaperman, author and radio commentator.

nostrils. The short man had been through all this before. He had come there to eat, and he never missed a course. But between them, he dozed placidly and belched audibly into the great bulge of his shirt front, which covered his chin. He had come there for the real business of the evening, and not for the commercials. Both he and the tall man had had a very good time.

TAPE 21
(May 15, 1953)

About the time of the ending of the First World War, a series of circumstances quickly following upon each other brought me closer to my aunt and her ménage than I had ever been before. My mother had been a widow for many years and I had been away at school so that I had only seen my mother and my aunt intermittently during this period. At the time of the war, I had been asked by the Office of Naval Intelligence to supervise the inspection of all camouflaged vessels entering the ports of the Eighth Naval District, the headquarters of which were in New Orleans.

In the meantime, my aunt and her husband had decided to come from the country[41] to live in New Orleans, where his death occurred within a few months of that of my mother. Thus she was left to live entirely alone and shortly thereafter she became totally blind. Throughout these sightless years and until the end, she would abruptly cut short any discussion of the possibility of an operation. Moreover, any reference to this affliction made in her presence was more than pointedly ignored.

Except for a caretaker living in one room, the old house[42] in the country had been unoccupied by any member of the family for over fifteen years. It was an estate of ordinary disrepair, but intact. "Intact" means that all of the parts were there and simply had to be replaced and water and heat

---

[41]Lafayette.

[42]Old house meaning The Shadows.

and light put in. How we'd ever escaped the gingerbread remodeling of the last half of the last century, I cannot understand. When its ownership fell into my hands, I found it to be a simple and lovely old place, not inconveniently situated too far from the country and indissolubly linked not only with my own childhood but that of my mother and my aunt. I lived here alone and my aunt continued to live alone in New Orleans. When I went there, at first, I had a room at a club, but spent almost as much time under her roof as I did downtown. She was deeply attached to me as far back as I can remember, and she simply could not understand this arrangement.

As her infirmity worsened, I felt that I could not help but stay with her, entirely, on my trips to New Orleans. I dislike traveling one foot, but I went to the point of taking an appointment of giving talks on painting there every two weeks just so that I could see her that often. She would not admit it to herself, but she was very lonely. She had house guests and people in and out all the time. These people were very kind to her in her last years. This was what was called living alone. What she meant was that she would tolerate no regular paid companion. Anyway, none of them could have stood the gaff for very long.

Until the very last, the sound of the doorbell in her ears was like the sound of the gong to the firehorse. She received everyone. It made her very happy to receive as often as she could the people whom she liked. It made her very happy, too, at times to receive the people she didn't like. There was always the possibility, if not the probability, of a difference of opinion and she liked nothing better than that. She gloried in independence, but only when it was her own. You will have found this picture of her last environment very necessary, not only because cooking springs intimately from environment, but because for these final thirty years there came into her life the perfect instrument for the realization of her cuisine and her personality inherently rich in compassion.

TAPE 22
(May 22, 1953)

(Thirty one years ago today, I moved back to this old house after an absence of fifteen years.)

When my aunt moved to New Orleans from the country, she brought with her her own cook. Her name was Celimene Burns.[43] I used this spelling because it has been used before in connection with her. Because Celimene was the heroine of Moliere's play *Le Misanthrope,* and because whatever the origin of the last name, the first name usually took some French form whether historical or fictional, and was much more euphonious. I know of several people who have taken to collecting these very lovely French first names, for they are fast dying out.

My aunt had bought a lot with houses on a corner so that there could be two entrances. There was her house on the corner. Behind it and detached was a garage and behind this, separate from either, was a house for Celimene. Thus, she had her own house and her own private entrance to it, and she could see whomsoever she wished and have stay with her anybody she wished for as long as she wanted them to. During my aunt's later sightless years, she could not, very naturally, bear to be alone.

It was only when my aunt had house guests with whom

---

[43]Celimene Burns was from Lafayette.

49

she could occupy herself that Celimene had any rest at all. I do not actually believe that her health would have stood the strain if she had not had this separate small house to go back to. Now Celimene Burns was a superlative cook. That is the reason for these words. She was employed as a cook and a maid of all work, getting what help she could from the successive chauffeurs, whom she, herself, picked out and employed. She delighted to plan things, manage them, and then do all the work herself. My aunt disliked being touched, and the ordeal of dressing her and taking care of her from head to foot fell to Celimene and Celimene alone. Indeed, at the last, she would take orders from Celimene that she would flatly refuse to take from her trained nurses. And please remember, all this time, she was cooking. People were coming in, as it happened to be around dinner time; extra trays had to be prepared.

During these latter years, she was so enfeebled that she could not go into the dining room and, during her waking hours, she was confined to a great and immovable arm chair in her bedroom. When any old friend was asked for dinner with her, they were brought two identical trays on two small tables and set before them, while I took the man in my room, and was served exactly the same way. This service was exactly as it would have been at the dining room table, but being divided into, say, four parts, it became a great deal more complicated for Celimene after the arduous duties of her day.

It was all contrived, of course, because my aunt could not be allowed to realize that her limitations interfered in the slightest with the regular routine of her household. On the other hand, I believe that it gratified Celimene to continue to create the same things which she had served these same people for many years. If my aunt did not remember what they especially liked, Celimene did. Many years before all this, my aunt had made it a custom to have two dinners a year, one on Christmas and one on her birthday, to which she asked, almost invariably, the same two groups of her very old friends. As time passed, every year, one or two chairs would have been vacant except that some substitution had to be made which would be the least noticeable. It was a delicate problem until the force of circumstances made it possible to end it by having some one of her old friends have a small and intimate dinner with her in her room.

TAPE 23
(May 29, 1953)

It is always difficult to build a picture of the interaction between two personalities. And the personalities of which I speak were very much to themselves, as there was not the usual families to surround them. The question of employer and employee in the rigid sense of the term simply did not seem to exist. Celimene had her kind of security and through this my aunt developed her own sense of security. Their interdependence was so great and so mutual that either thought that they were independent of the other. They were both in their different ways gregarious to a degree. Sherwood Anderson,[44] who delighted in her gumbo, said that she literally ate people up. She had her own ideas about conventionality. She once told me the story that before a great convention of her church,[45] a distinguished committee had called upon her to say that certain households in New Orleans had been allotted the care of two bishops during the convention. She said at once, "You know that these various bishops have been billeted with families. You know, and everybody knows, that I live here alone. You know, too, that I cannot have two men seen entering my house after a

---

[44]Sherwood Anderson (1876-1941). Famous American author whose naturalist novels and short stories portray life in the small towns of midwestern America.

[45]Her church was an Episcopal congregation.

late night session, even if each bore on his back a boldly lettered placard with the words, 'I am a bishop.' "

On the other hand was this kind of thing: Celimene's large kitchen windows and large back porch were not more than six or eight feet from the sidewalk of the side street. She knew everybody and everybody knew her. No one would pass without a hail to them or a hail from them. There have followed conversations which immediately afterward reached my aunt more quickly than even the radio news could have reached her. Celimene knew the daughters and granddaughters and small nieces and cousins of all her friends, and she was most particularly proud of their achievements in school. She managed to keep an eye on those who were beginning their studies of music. She knew that at the other end of the house was my aunt, in her big chair, alone and fiddling with the radio dial. She knew that in the next room to her was a grand piano which was always silent. I never knew why it was there and never asked.

Celimene would ask one or two of these children to go home, put up their school books, dress and come back and that she would have something for them. Shortly afterwards, they came back, impeccably starched and resplendent with large bows in their hair. She would take them into my aunt and tell her who they were and that they were now old enough to sing a little bit and to play the piano a little bit. Soon, from the other room would come the hesitant tinkling of the piano and the shrill piping voices which we all know, with my aunt bravely calling for encores. My aunt seemed always refreshed by this brief and simple relief of her tedium, and the recitalists were profoundly refreshed by large hunks of homemade ice cream, part of which they were to take to their parents. Nothing that I can say can reveal more poignantly the relationship between my aunt and Celimene.

TAPE 24
(May 30, 1953)

My aunt took Celimene everywhere with her. She did not like to travel, but once, when her doctor told my aunt that Celimene had developed what was described to me as a spot on her lung, my aunt dropped everything and took her for three months to Denver. When she took the small house on the Pacific coast, she took with her Celimene as personal maid and housekeeper. When she went to New York especially to see the theatre, she took Celimene there, too. She could not go out to restaurants, and she tired very soon of hotel food. She went to the theatre every night that she could. One morning, she told Celimene that unless she could have a gumbo, she was going home. Celimene was at a loss, until finally, she asked my aunt for five dollars and disappeared. She came back within a few hours to the room with a large can of gumbo and a can of rice made as only we in this region can make it. I have said that Celimene knew everybody; she did. She had gone up to Harlem and found a family there from the same small town from which my aunt and Celimene had gone to New Orleans. The moment that these kind people heard that my aunt wanted the gumbo, it was no sooner said than done. They had everything, including fresh filé, which is compounded of dried sassafras leaves. (If this preparation can only be bought in large bottles, always divide it into very small ones in order that the aroma may not escape into the air inside the bottle.) My aunt would only stay there as long as she could have this freshly prepared for her.

54

The only thing which my aunt liked which came from the hotel kitchens were the croissants. I tried to explain to her that this was a commercial pastry, but nothing must do but I must search high and wide for the receipt and she was never satisfied with the homemade results of it. I remember, very vividly, a week's trip with them to Havana, which is only a day or so out of New Orleans. I got up very early, and I went down to my aunt's room on another floor. I had thought that I was early, but she'd awakened Celimene and sent her to some great market around the corner to buy every sort of tropical fruit, which meant of course, any fruit which Celimene had never seen before. My aunt sat in a chair by the window. On the right side of the chair was a table, and on the left side of the chair was another table. On the left-hand table was a large pile of tropical fruit with one bite taken out of each. On the right-hand table was a large pile of tropical fruit, as yet intact. In the center of it was my aunt, covered by a large napkin and determined to go through the whole ordeal only to be able to say that none of it was worth anything.

The only Sunday of this stay in Havana happened to be Communion Sunday. Now, at home, my aunt tried never to miss this special service. And at home, Celimene made the Communion bread for her own church, and also never missed this service. On this particular Sunday, after my aunt was dressed for church, she begged Celimene to dress and to go to church with her. Afterwards, she insisted that Celimene go with her to the only Communion rail open to them in the whole city. There is no point to it, except that it was the most natural thing in the world.

TAPE 25
(May 30, 1953)

My aunt used to write me here or telephone me here at about the season of the year when the days were filled with smoky haze and the nights were likely to end in a hard frost. Her letters, whatever else they might be about, always concluded with, "Can you find me some good pork sausage? Can't you get me the new cane syrup?" I would canvass the stores here in town and look far afield to find and to send to her every kind that I could. Her reply was always, "Thank you, my dear, for sending the sausage; it was horrible!" This came from my once sharing with her some country sausage which had been sent to me as a present. I wish that I had never let her have it, because such was its perfection that it was never again duplicated.

The same pleas from her would come to me to the country here for each season's new cane syrup. You went around and you bought every possible can, with every possible label, and you shipped it to her. She also thanked you for this and she also said it was pretty bad. Now the secret of all this I didn't catch onto for years. She did not want the new cane syrup for herself. She wanted to send it on to other people in the North. She confessed to me secretly once, that she liked maple syrup much better, but I noted that she never ate it before anybody. Such was her secret gastronomic loyalty to the late Confederacy.

The southern part of the state of Louisiana has always been very proud of its oysters, either raw or cooked, just as

Maryland is very proud of certain seafoods edible there. For some years, the availability, in perfection, of such food from the water has been deeply affected by the tremendous development in the oil industry, both inshore and offshore. The State Department, through conservation, has done, and is doing, great work in preventing future limitations in seafood. Both inshore and offshore, the by-products or wastage from oil wells, as well as from the gasses of innumerable gasoline motors, has defiled the waters by destroying the wealth of natural vegetation upon which the fish feed. Another factor has been the vast and necessary systems of drainage canals, inland, in order to avoid periodic general floods. The salinity of the seawater which nature had maintained as a perfect balance for millions of years has thus, suddenly, been upset. There seems to be no perceptible dearth of seafood. But the trouble of getting to it and the expense of marketing it has risen enormously.

We still have oyster loaves. These were sometimes called "Peace-makers" because the tardy husbands coming in late at night would stop at some night cafe and have them made, and bring them home, very fresh and very hot, to their wives. The top was cut from a loaf of bread and saved. Both were put in the oven and toasted slightly inside and brushed with garlic butter. In the meantime, any number of oysters had been fried and then, on the first, they were put inside with olives and pickles and things like that, covered with the toasted top of the bread, wrapped up in several layers of paper to keep them hot, and brought home. The effect of these somewhat tangible manifestations of guilt had to be nicely calculated. Everything hung upon the wife's appetite.

TAPE 26
(May 30, 1953)

The common and ultimate end of both my aunt and Celimene was perfection on the table. Therefore, everything had to come from Celimene's kitchen. Of course, there were patty shells which came from a dealer, but only because said things always come from a dealer. On the first really cold day of the oyster season, my aunt would call in Celimene for a discussion about the present season's oysters. Were they large or small? And did they have, at this early stage, any taste at all? And so on and so on. It finally wound up by Celimene saying that they were large, and they were a good size for frying. The portent being auspicious, my aunt agreed to officially open the bi-valve season at lunch the next day. She added that she was delighted at the seasonal change because she hadn't had oysters, it seemed, in years, and hadn't been able to give her guests the marvelous fried oysters which came from Celimene's kitchen.

During the winter season, she would occasionally have one or two intimate friends in for Sunday night supper. And she'd always go into the thing of what they wanted and what they were going to have and all that. Now, what my aunt did not know was that about a block behind her house was a small beer and oyster parlor, which made the best fried oysters in all the world. They were luscious in spite of their gigantic size. They evidently had been bred and trained to shrink not one iota from their fiery destiny, nor afterwards would they shed one speck of oil upon their plates. My aunt did not know that people drove from miles, all over New Orleans, to surround these things. Celimene could almost always duplicate a miracle, but she was confronted here with defeat. When most of the food was ready, she would hie herself to this joint with a hot and airtight container swathed in cloth, and come back with a harvest. The usual compliments about the oysters were lost to the usual compliments about the other things which came from her kitchen.

All went well that winter, until one fateful day, when my aunt specified to Celimene these fried oysters, among other things, for some people who were expected. At the strategic moment, Celimene telephoned the alchemist that she wanted so many dozen fried oysters to be ready at such and such an instance. To her horror, he replied that he had no fried oysters left at all. Indeed, not even any oysters large enough to meet his standard for frying, but that he had left only some smaller very good, raw oysters, which might be used for other things. She had no time. She sent someone for these at once. In the meantime, she prepared, as best she could, to fry them herself. Fortunately, the people came late and there was time enough for everything. Fortunately, the other man and myself were having food on trays in another room, so that I did not see her face as she and this first and last oyster became as much one as they would ever be.

After the people had left, the postmortem was a long and wonderful one. My aunt said, "Celimene, everybody who has come here knows that you can fry oysters beyond compare. Everybody also knows that they are larger and better than anyone else can have. These little things you had for dinner today must have come already fried, at the last moment, from some restaurant in the neighborhood. Now, if you cannot make the usual large fried oysters, tell me beforehand and we'll put in something else." I passed Celimene the high sign of eternal silence and my aunt always had perfection after that, though she did not know where it came from. Celimene was a good scout.

TAPE 27
(Coronation Day in London. June 2, 1953)

(This tape, I believe, will prove imperfect. I shall correct it as far as possible.)

Those whom my aunt liked, she liked enormously, especially her old friends. Those whom she did not like simply did not exist, and she showed it. When I say that she received everybody, I mean that she received those who got past the front door and Celimene. When others got in, it was always by prearrangement. If my aunt did not find out from them what she wanted, their leave was made very short. Celimene was always instructed to observe how her visitors were dressed. The very next day, she would always call these people up and tell them how pleased she was to have seen them, and how well they looked, and certain details of their dress, which Celimene had reported to her. Blindness was never mentioned.

However, this sort of thing sometimes worked the other way. My aunt could not see whether her guest had left the room and left the house. Therefore, my aunt and Celimene contrived a system of signals. When someone rose and was about to go, she would ring for Celimene to show them out. Celimene would stand immediately behind the large chair in which my aunt sat, and kept her finger concealed in the folds of the shoulder of my aunt's dress. As long as there was silence and the finger was there, my aunt simply made conversation. When the finger was lifted, my aunt took it for granted that the people had left the room and left the house.

On one occasion, Celimene had to leave my aunt's chair and the protection of the finger and stoop to pick up something of this woman, who was leaving. My aunt, who had no sense of time, as the blind have not, said to Celimene, "Has old pineapple legs gone?" She was still about six feet from my aunt, in front of a mirror, putting on her hat. My aunt was tired and petulant and I believe she completely denied that she'd ever said any such thing, or denied that it could ever have been overheard. At any rate, she knew that she would make up for this thing a hundred times later, and so did Celimene, and nothing was said about the thing afterward, at all.

TAPE 29[46]
(Undated)

(This tape appears to be a "scrapbook" compiled from diverse scraps of tapes which further describe the management of Weeks Hall's aunt's household.)

It is with regret that I must so often speak of my aunt's blindness. Throughout her life, it was so much a part of her that it was never even mentioned. That was all right, but in trying in some way (to explain) the connection between her and Celimene, it (her blindness) cannot be omitted because there was the cause, the very root of their mutual loyalty. Because she ignored it, we must ignore it. But everything about her was imbued in this almost silent obligato.

(The tape is so disjointed that a portion has been omitted for the sake of coherency.)

Celimene was a great favorite and rightly so. Through her enormous network of information she would find out who was ill and in what hospital. Despite her strict attention to details of management at home, she would find time, always, to cook exactly the right things for the right people and take these trays to them. Whether it were my aunt's friends in private hospitals or her own friends and relations at Charity Hospital, she would never fail to do this. Hospital

---

[46]Tape 28 was erased.

food may best be described in Swinburne's phrase, "pale beyond porch or portal," and the sight of the starched Celimene coming in with a large tray smelling like heaven itself and surmounted by her flashing smile was a sight never to be forgotten, nor the gratitude for it forgotten, even long, long afterward. It was part of Celimene and of my aunt to do these things continually and they gloried in it.

TAPE 30
(June 6, 1953)

As a child, I had had no family Christmases in the big house in the country. And later, I had had no family Christmases when I lived, for several years, with the two Creole ladies in the big, old twenty-two room house in New Orleans. After that, I was away at school and, of course, there could be no family Christmases then. Widely separated for various reasons, my widowed mother and my widowed aunt and myself had never been together for Christmas.

Now, only my aunt was left, and I was determined to make this feast for her every year. This meant coming down to the city from the country where I now lived and bringing with me one of my men, who had been trained in table service. It took some days before to get each thing which was wanted from each separate dealer, which my aunt and Celimene judged to have this product in perfection. It took a whole day for preparation. I won't explain how difficult this was. By chance, my aunt had bought a house on one floor. When the front door was opened, and you stood in one spot, you could see into exactly nine rooms. The doors to these rooms were always open because my aunt could never abide a closed door. Aside from all this, she was determined to hear what she could not see. The numberless visitors to her on Christmas day could also hear what they could not see. They would have to be brought little cakes and wine, the fresh black coffee, everytime they came. And through all these visits, my aunt would certainly pay no attention to her present guests—she would ring the bell for Celimene and unashamedly give her directions or ask her questions about the progress in the kitchen.

Now every Christmas day opened with a rite. Celimene would get up very early and start the Christmas morning eggnog, which was to be shared by everyone under her roof. While my aunt was still asleep, we would all silently go upstairs and get the concealed Christmas presents for everybody and pile them on the dining room table, which would scarcely hold them all. Nobody had been forgotten. Celimene, in the meantime, had wakened my aunt and dressed her in a Chinese vermillion dressing gown. And with her white hair and her school-girl complexion at eighty, she was radiant. She became more radiant still, when she was led into the dining room and put into a chair, and one opened the presents, while the other put the cards down and said what they were. Her curiosity and her pleasure was that of a child.

I remember one Christmas with a touching note. Celimene had hired a man from New Iberia to be chauffeur.[47] This boy had never before had a room to himself. Celimene had put new linoleum on the floor, arranged curtains, and small things like that and, indeed, it was his first home which he could call a home. While he was helping my aunt with things, he suddenly burst into tears and ran into the kitchen. I didn't know what was the matter. When I went to find out, all he could say was, "Well, she's so happy, that's all." These few words he said to me were the straight stuff, unmarred by the tinsel and glitter of any season.

---

[47]Clement Knatt who is presently employed at the Shadows.

TAPE 31[48]
(June 6, 1953)

My aunt had always been fastidious in her dress, and she had always sought them (her clothing) at the same couturiére. This woman, who sent her buyers regularly twice a year to Paris, had not left her shop to go to Canal Street, to the center of town, twenty blocks away, for twenty years. My aunt would shop with her by telephone, depending entirely upon this woman's taste and exact knowledge of each small change in fashion. Boxes and boxes of these recommended dresses would be sent to my aunt's house. She could only feel them and the dressmaker would discuss, over the telephone, what each dress looked like, and from these she kept what she wanted.

(Re-occurring breaks altered the coherency of this tape and a portion has again been omitted.)

Sightless and with advancing age, she sought refuge in the chair and the radio from which it was difficult to arouse her or to get her to order the new things which she needed yearly. The story about the gloves is a good one. When my aunt could go out at all, she would telephone someone and ask them to go to church with her, if the weather was right.

One Sunday morning, through the closed door of my room, I heard a tremendous discussion about what seemed

---

[48]Tape 31 is extremely disarrayed. Obvious breaks in the tape are noted.

to be gloves. Celimene told my aunt that she could not go to church in the gloves that she had been wearing. She told her that she had burned them. She told my aunt that time and time again she had asked her for time enough to go downtown and get several pairs of gloves for her, but somehow it had seemed that there had never been time. My aunt replied with finality that she could not go to church. Celimene replied that the very next day she would go downtown and get all the gloves which my aunt wanted, but in the meantime, she had out in her room a perfectly brand-new pair of black kid gloves which had been given her several years before by Miss Blank in New York. She had never worn them and the package had only been opened to show them to people. Celimene went out and got the new gloves. My aunt put them on, saying that she had never had gloves which fitted her like these before. And she went on, in a proper state of mind for church.

The next day and many days after, she could not find time to go downtown to buy gloves for my aunt, until a later Sunday, through my same closed door, I heard the discussion all over again. My aunt wanted these gloves. She would give Celimene any amount of money to buy others for herself, but these black kid gloves fitted her as none had ever done before and Celimene could get whatever gloves she wanted for both of them.

TAPE 32
(June 8, 1953)

Whatever happened, I used to telephone my aunt from my house here in the country to her house in New Orleans every night. I almost never had anything to report from here, but she was always voluble and I loved it. The insistent call of the telephone bell usually means tidings of arrivals, and therefore I seldom answer them. This begins the story, which I later told a distinguished and sensitive writer, who made from it a classic. In my poor words, it simply becomes a recounting of facts, and because it shows uniquely the relationship between my aunt and Celimene.

One day here in the country, about noon, the telephone set up such a clamor so I felt that I must answer it. It was my aunt calling over long distance from New Orleans. Simply to hear her voice was of course reassurance, but that voice was but a ghost of itself. It was not illness, but the fact that she had had a stenographer for the day and that stenographer could not find, among her thousands of receipts, the receipt for sour oranges. I replied that Celimene had it and made this thing for her every year and put them up into jars. She then said that when she asked Celimene for it, not being able to find it written down, Cleimene had said, "You know, when you gave me that receipt, which takes days to make, you made me swear that I would never in my life give it to anyone. I will make it for your own use every year, but nobody but me is going to have that receipt."

My aunt then implored me to telephone this very dear

68

friend of hers, a member of the McIlhenny family who lived on Avery Island. This receipt there was kept very secret also, but it was at once sent to my aunt. When she found her own mislaid copy of the receipt, it was in exactly the same wording and it must have been exchanged between the two families a century before.

Shortly after, about this time, the trees must have commenced to disappear, either because they were attacked by some pest which rapidly decimated them, or because the preserves, from which they were made, took too long and too much skill to make properly. Through my aunt's spies, agents and informers, she finally found, near the mouth of the Mississippi River, a large grove of commercial oranges. This was surrounded, strange to say, by a long line of sour oranges, which took no more trouble to spray at the same time as the commercial oranges. She had struck uranium, and I honestly believe that she bought far more crates of these sour oranges than she actually needed, simply because she would not take the chance that anyone else might have the chance of making these sour orange preserves. I wouldn't put it past her for a minute!

Those in the kitchen approached this preserving season with dread. I don't blame them. You had first to grate off every shred of the rind and then, as I remember it, they were put alternately for days or hours into baths of lime water and of brine.

Then the pulp was taken out and thrown away. On the stove there had to be other things added, especially a certain kind of vanilla. All this then had to be poured into waiting preserve jars labeled with my aunt's name and dated like a vintage. They were best at two or three years, she said. The jars actually seemed to sparkle with an amber clarity as they were put away to wait their turn to be opened. They were used as a dessert only for my aunt's special company, or they were given, one by one, wrapped in what Celimene called "silk paper," to those only whom my aunt wanted to show honor, much as the legendary golden rose is given by the

Pope to those royal women whom he considers due this respect. I hope that Celimene will keep this receipt in her heart. I hope that she will bequeath it to the Library of Congress. There's something left out, of course, to prove that she had always been a very good cook.

TAPE 37[49]
(June 23, 1953)

Coming to my aunt's house very late one rainy afternoon, I threw my wet raincoat on the pantry table and followed it with the wet packages. I heard the radio going on from my aunt's room on the other side of the house, and on the kitchen side of the pantry door there came the conversation and gay laughter of Celimene's friends. They loved to come and see her and, in return, she loved to have them. I happen to know that, that day, on one side of the back of the stove was a large pot of turtle soup just waiting for the dinner hour and the pungency of its cloves permeated the house. That was one thing.

But there was another thing, another aroma which came through this door, which I could not at once identify. It drew me into the kitchen like a magnet. After the usual amenities, for I knew all of these few people, I asked Celimene, "What have you in that pot on this side of the stove?" She said, "Spare ribs. You know, I have Mrs. Torian's turtle soup ready and I was just waiting for you. In the meantime, I'm making some spare ribs for my friends here. Don't you want to try a little bit?"

Now, Celimene made certain things for my aunt. She also made certain things for the kitchen, which never got past the

---

[49]Tapes 33, 34, 35 and 36 were unavailable.

71

pantry door. This was one of them. In painting, occasionally you do things which are accidents of perfection; you cannot do them again, or as well, to save your life. I had always heard of spare ribs as being a sort of something which you bought because there was nothing left that day to market at that time. I had always associated them, too, with a word such as Edmund Longshanks. He was royal, but I cannot imagine a man with a royal presence with a name like that. She scraped a few shreds of crisp meat and the meat which adhered to the bone itself into a saucer for me. This was royal, despite any lowly name it bore. I brought all this up because I believe that it is a story which illustrates the origin of "haute cuisine." It all sprang from lowly cooking. This mixture, developed, which I think is a perfectly good word, by a great chef with a flair for improvisation, can become one of the great dishes of the world. Exactly the right pastries must be found for it, and exactly the right proportions of dressings or vegetables. The basis of this perfection was home cooking. All that it would take to make a great and named dish was training and disciplined imagination.

TAPE 38
(Undated)

In speaking of complicated dishes of the great school, I remember that I had in the room next to me, for years, what was probably the first edition of "Franquescatti," who was Queen Victoria's chef. I kept it because I would want to show some of my friends a formula for Christmas punch. I referred to this book for some guidance once, and here is what I found. The first lines were: "Take twelve quarts of brandy." Then it went on for, oh, perhaps two inches, two inches and a half, and wound up with: "Let mull one year." At last I sent it to my aunt in New Orleans as curiosa for her collection of cookbooks, and because it had belonged to my grandmother. It has disappeared from her effects, and I cannot see what use this kind of thing can be to anyone. The Prince of Wales is the first gentleman of Europe. He must have had to go to many state banquets, and how he and his tailor ever got together after these enormous quantities of food had affected his figure, I cannot understand. I should like to have this book now, only to see the illustrations and to find out what I suppose any chef in any large hotel could tell you, that is, what the word "remous,"[50] used as a noun, is.

The illustrations for these enormous creations were

---

[50]"Remous", used as a noun, could mean a utensil used in stirring.

woodcuts which reminded you of involved piping, such as the greatest oil refinery in the world at Baton Rouge, or the old illustrations of the Mardi Gras parades, or the delightful and long-gone Rube Goldberg cartoons. Every bone shank was covered by dozens of paper pantalettes, and where careful support was needed, I suppose curly-cues, mashed potatoes, and cut flowers of radishes, and things like that, covered the whole thing. I imagine that the chef set himself the problem of making everything edible look unlike what it was and to build something which seemed to defy the laws of gravitation. The long, ornamented skewers running through these whole things helped very greatly to produce this effect. There is still downstairs two very early volumes of Fox's *Book of Martyrs*. The woodcuts in it are incredible. It was my childhood joy to take these out on a rainy afternoon and look at people being drawn and quartered by horses, people being eviscerated, people strung up by their thumbs or by their toes, people with their heads being cut off, people being roasted alive, and all that sort of thing. These things so much resembled the woodcut illustrations of the joints of beef and cattle that I saw little difference between the old cookbook and the old *Book of Martyrs*.

TAPE 39
(June 28, 1953)

I had repeatedly been asked how did my aunt get Celimene, as though you could go back somewhere and take another one off the shelf. I have already said that during the last year of the First World War, I was in New Orleans, both because my mother was very ill and because I was in the naval service there. This was also the year that my aunt and her husband moved to New Orleans from the country, bringing Celimene with them. It was my first prolonged contact with Celimene. I have never asked either my aunt or Celimene how she came into my aunt's service. It was their business. I found her there and I was very grateful that she was still with my aunt until she died thirty or more years later.

Celimene was ambitious and loyal and very intelligent. This was the raw material, wherever it came from. With my aunt's approaching total blindness, she became, in very truth, my aunt's alter ego and anticipated every need. I do not mean to say that this would have occurred with any other employer and Celimene, but it did exist here. Everything happened to be right, and in exactly the right proportions. Try to make a simple salad here, and you find that you cannot do it. You can get exactly the right oil to mix in the right proportions, with the right wine vinegar and a pinch of salt and pepper, but you cannot get in the country here, for some reason, the right kind of lettuce on which to pour this mixture to the exact point where it will be properly marinated. The French, of course, would have a word for it—indefinable and yet precise. The word is "se marier." A paradox is that it may as well apply to totally contrasting things as well as to totally sympathetic things. My aunt took as much pride in Celimene's services to her as Celimene did in her loyalty to those services. When no one was in the house to whom my aunt could talk, the bell which I had placed on the table beside her was rung a hundred times a day for Celimene. It may have been rung ten times over to ask Celimene the same questions but she always came; she was there.

TAPE 40
(Undated)

The doctor had told me many months before, and later he had had to force practical nurses on duty in order that Celimene could get any sleep at all, as she was called for by my aunt at all hours, night and day. Later, when special nurses had to be called in, in her blindness, she called them all Celimene. When the angel of death came on duty that night, she was prim and starched and accustomed. Celimene, on the other hand, sat huddled in her chair and she could only answer to anyone who asked her anything, "She don't call me anymore, she don't call me anymore."

And she never did again. Five minutes before the ceremonies, the next day, I asked that Celimene be brought to my room. I bade her go at once to the foot of my aunt's coffin and remain there above everybody else. When I came into the room, the services began immediately, and Celimene rode with me and a few others in the automobile going to my aunt's grave. There was no question in the matter. My aunt would have wanted it so.

TAPE 42 [51]
(Undated)

Now, in the latter part of the seventeenth century, on the margin of the coast of Louisiana, there were two cultures in existence. The first was the Gaelic European, who had brought with him a tradition of cookery and a few pitiful seeds and plants which were unequally raised with success in the new environment. The other culture came from the western coast of Africa and was brought in by the Spaniards in the ruthless sixteenth century in order that they might be used as the labor of the owners of the land. The Spaniards were shrewd enough to import these unfortunate humans into the lower part of the United States, because that latitude was already about the same as the latitude which they had just been forced to leave. Otherwise, you might have had a more equal distribution. This was also all mixed up with the Hamilton and Jefferson idea. One was for industrialism and the other was for the rural idea. The rivalry finally exploded into the Civil War.

To get back to cooking, Thomas Morphy, in general, puts it very well. Here were two distinct groups of people, each coming from lands far apart, and each never having known the customs of the other. They came into a land which was practically a wilderness, except for what primitive dishes the

---

[51]Tape 41 was unavailable.

American Indian had developed for his mere subsistence. Each group had had its own traditional cookery, one much simpler than the other. Most of all, in this new land, they found that they could or could not raise things which were very necessary to the cooking which they had had back home, across the sea. It took a little genius, the genius of improvisation, which is sometimes higher than the talent for mere planned art, to make out of these new factors an entirely new and delightful form of cooking. Some of the old things could be grown in the New World. For substitutes, other native horticultural products were substituted. It was to these cooks alone that an entirely different style, in the French term, developed. And everything goes to their credit. It is strange that the only original jazz music and the only original cooking came from New Orleans and these are considered abroad now as the only indigenous native things which America has contributed to the world. So much for my trying to find the origins of these receipts.

TAPE 43
(June 11, 1953)

The most elaborate cooking was always found in the greater houses. The West was as yet undeveloped, and the people along the Atlantic seaboard copied the furnishings and the customs of England as the different tastes developed, from the purer Federal influence in the last century to the bulbous Victorian influence in the middle of the last century. Salem, Massachusetts and Portsmouth, New Hampshire are examples of what a short and great upsurge in industrialism, due to the whaling industry, could do for the perfection of architecture and furnishings.

I repeat, in the South, when you think of it, the great houses followed the great crops. In Maryland, you had rye and whiskey. In Virginia, you had whiskey and tobacco. In North Carolina and Charleston, and in South Carolina and Savannah, you had rice. Then, you came over a rather sterile patch and up into Kentucky you had horses and whiskey. In Natchez, you were surrounded by enormous acreages of cotton, for which Mobile was a port. Along the Bayou Teche country in southern Louisiana, you had the export of all these things. Besides this, it brought down, through the Ohio River, by water, all of the products of the fast-growing Middle West. These found an outlet through the mouth of the Mississippi and also through the mouth of the Mississippi came in so much imported material directly from France. It became our first truly cosmopolitan city. The cooking there, though basically Gaelic, had been affected by food which was attracted to high Spanish seasoning, to various delicate nuances of American Indian cooking, especially the corn dishes, and most of all, by the Negro cooks, who had contrived with almost genius to combine all these factors. To say nothing of all this, in the country close by were the fish and the waters of the Gulf and there were the seasonal dishes, such as "Crawfish Bisque" in the spring and myriads of oysters in the winter.

TAPE 44
(Undated)

These oysters were especially combined with rice, in the winter season, in the special dishes found seldom elsewhere. Aside from its gumbos, Louisiana is probably known best for our especially cooked rice and our especially dripped black coffee than any other dishes. The rice came to us from the eastern lowlands of Asia. Coffee came to us from the uplands of southwest Asia through our French colonization, both in the raw grain and in raw bean. Since the coffee bean cannot be propagated here, it came into any port, but probably New Orleans, where so much of it was used. Rice, on the other hand, was imported into the ports of Charleston and of Georgia because the lowlands surrounding these ports duplicated the paddies of Asia and rice could be grown commercially thereabouts. Rice soon found its way to the lowlands of southwest Louisiana, where it is a large commercial crop growing under the same conditions in which it does in China.

Here is the little-known reason for chicory being added to coffee now both in Paris and in New Orleans. When the British fleet blockaded the continent of Europe during the Napoleonic wars, no coffee could be imported on the continent. The people then began using roasted chicory root as a beverage in place of coffee. After 1815, they continued to use the chicory mixed with coffee as they preferred the taste, and the economy, of the compounded beverage, particularly when it was thick in making and stirred in hot milk. The practice then continued until this day.

The custom was brought to New Orleans and other cities on the Mexican Gulf after 1815. The Acadians and those who settled in the southwest Louisiana section before 1790 used strong coffee and have never used chicory. We used pure coffee here, in vacuum cans, without chicory. With us in the Acadian country here, very strongly fresh-dripped coffee is a wine of conversation and of business. I imagine that 90% of the business deals, big and little, in this parish are conducted over successive cups of this coffee. In the homes, the equipment, and the equipment must be very exact, is always on the back of the stove and every visitor, of no matter what station, joins in this brew. Incidentally, I always think of the universal potatoes as a sort of trailer to any food which is served, whereas rice is a catalyst. Not affecting the food which lies upon it, it merely enriches it with a sort of supreme and crystalline purity.

TAPE 45

A TAPE TO EDMOND SOUCHON[52]
(September, 1954)

Dear Edmond,

The tape which you just sent me stimulated me, as your father's pictures always did. It has led me into a train of thought, and into memories of Bunk Johnson,[53] here, in the last ten years of his life in New Iberia. Every now and then, someone passes through here and asks me about him, and asks where he is buried.

Many years ago, the Russian ballet under Diaghilev[54] produced for a time a short ballet which they had titled, "Le Tambeau de Couperin." It was a simple tribute to that musician of the late French Renaissance. This kind of thing is reminiscent of the needlework memorial pictures which were done a century or so ago. They were always symbolic and always contained a weeping willow tree and a mourner. These sparse recollections of Bunk and his last days are likewise meant to be a small tribute.

---

[52]Dr. Edmon Souchon, II (1897-1968). He was a New Orleans surgeon, musician, author and jazz authority.

[53]William Geary "Bunk" Johnson (1879-1949). World famous black jazz musician.

[54]Sergei Pavlovich Diaghilev (1872-1929). Famous Russian ballet, art and music impresario.

He died, I think, about seven or eight years ago. In a cemetery here, he lies buried under a concrete slab. Such is the tempo of our times, that there is no name, no date, nothing. Such is the tempo of our times, that he rests here in anonymity and silence, I am sure, awaiting the first note of the last trumpet.

I never knew him in his early great days. He came to me in his early 30s, as a yardman. His own terms. I had, in those days, a beautiful, highly-bred, English setter. They became devoted to each other and Bunk suggested that she was too much of a lady to be fed canned dog food. Therefore, he started to cook her meals for her. He said that he was sure that she liked seasonings just as we did. I had no cook, and I let him go ahead. Be it as it may, there finally evolved an excellent hash, perfectly seasoned, and added to it were yellow grits. Right from the beginning, Spot shared these delightful breakfast briskets. She was as much addicted to black coffee as was Bunk. The whole thing turned out very satisfactorily all around.

Shortly after all this, Bunk had to leave. He was given a position to teach music at some of the schools here. When he worked for me, he came only occasionally when I needed him or when I could find him. In absences from this place, he evidently resorted to the cup to relieve the drabness and the monotony of life in a small town. These moments of fantasy must have reached such heights that the authorities would hold him for his own safekeeping. This must have been so, because now and then, I would have letters from the dungeons from him. These were not written in blood, but in the only materials available to him—in pencil, on toilet paper, with a period after every word so that he would not miss the end of a sentence. He wanted little—Picayune cigarettes or Bull Durham.

When he was on the place here, he would talk interminably of old times and Louis Armstrong and his association with those who are now the immortals in his field. There were no tape recorders then. At this time he had no trumpet. Nor could he have played one—he had no teeth. He would continually say that Louis Armstrong had promised him a set. During the sugarcane grinding season, he drove a cane truck, and once he caught me when I was standing at my front gate. He ran over to me and pulled something out of his pocket, wrapped in toilet paper.

He said that Louis had sent him his teeth, and that Louis was going to send him a trumpet. I asked him why he didn't wear these teeth. He said that in the truck they joggled around in his mouth, and that he couldn't eat with them because they hurt him. He was waiting for his trumpet so that he could punctuate his notes with them.

I lost track of him for a long time—he seemed to be out of town. And then it came to me that he had been rediscovered by some authority on jazz, and that he had got a trumpet from somewhere and was somewhere recording his early style, which he had not used for many years. On account of old associations, I was, of course, tremendously excited. A phoenix arisen from the embers. I felt that his long years of silence would be a blessing, perhaps. He was preserved from the diluting and sweetening of his original period. All this would prove to be latent. He would come back primitive, archaic and strong as he was at first. It proved to be so.

Well, I hadn't seen Bunk in a long, long time. One week, the current issue of *Time* came in, and going through the pictures at first, in the division on Music, there was Bunk's picture. There followed an account of his having given a concert at the Palace of the Legion of Honor, in San Francisco, and of his rediscovery and of his triumph there. It amused me to tell people here for a day or so that this town had at last made the columns of *Time* magazine. I was asked where and how. I told them that they would have to find it for themselves. I do not remember if anyone ever did. He was totally unknown at that time in his own home town.

As I have said, I hadn't heard from Bunk in a long time. In the next day or two, an enormous roll of papers containing an issue of *Time* magazine came from San Francisco to me by special delivery. These were all from Bunk, and with them was a letter from him. Bless him, he had remembered me first of all. The letter from him was typewritten and was in his usual style a period after every word. Every sentence began with a capital. He said that he was well, and he hoped that I was, and that he was sending me a lot of papers with articles about himself. He said that he was writing on a typewriter which he had got secondhand and he said that he had on one side of him a very strong cup of black coffee and that this, together with the bell of the typewriter at the end of the line, kept him awake. Here he was, midway between 60 and 70, and he had left an auditorium filled with wild acclaim and applause. He said that he was unaccustomed to the folks out there and felt uneasy and could I find some way to get him, out there in San Francisco, a job lawn-mowing.

This recital, of course, brought him into the national public eye. He had his own name band afterwards—the band which would draw no audience unless he himself were there. He commenced to make a good deal of money. He was totally indifferent to all this. He would appear or he wouldn't appear. He had the assurance of genius. In this, his attitude during his latter years reminded me of the latter years of John Barrymore. When he might have been making hundreds of dollars a week, sometimes he was back of the house here fishing in the Bayou Teche.

I remember on one rainy Saturday night, the telephone rang about ten o'clock. It was a woman representative of *Life* magazine, who wanted him to come to New Orleans so that they could have a double-page spread on Bunk. I told her that *Life* was very sophisticated, but not enough so to know that at ten o'clock on Saturday night it would be very hard to find Bunk and those of his ilk. She asked me if he had a telephone at his house. I said that that would be the last place, even if he had had a telephone, that she would find him on Saturday night. I advised her to telephone the Harlem Grill and the Social Club and that she would find him there, probably incoherent. He was there, and he was incoherent, but I had wanted her to find this out for herself. I didn't want to mix things up. The next day, he telephoned back from my house to this journalist, and arrangements were made, and I gave him money to go down for photographs in *Life*. I understand that he got off all right, but nobody ever saw him after that, so the photographs never appeared.

I went to his house the night that he was dying. The darkness, the dark figures in the shadows, and the silence of it all was not like Bunk at all. When he died, I wired *Time* and *Life*. The funeral was held up until a group of jazz connoisseurs could come down for it. I couldn't get to the funeral, but I sent flowers and loaned my driver and my automobile for the family, as an extra car. They all came around the next day and thanked me very, very nicely.

I never heard Bunk play with a band, but one night someone brought him here with his trumpet, a very valuable instrument, and he played for me alone. His only accompaniment was a pint of "Four Roses." As he warmed up, he told me that he had already banked a hundred thousand dollars. When he left, he borrowed five dollars. A pittance, indeed, for a private recital. The privilege was all mine.

He was a small man, with courtly manners, and white hair, and a skin like old aged walnut, and the kindest, gentlest eyes I have ever seen in a human face.

May he rest in peace.

Index
(Prepared by John Raphael)